Little Women

Louisa May Alcott

Young Readers' Classics

Abridgement by
Barbara Greenwood

Illustrations by Greg Ruhl

KEY PORTER BOOKS

Canadian Cataloguing in Publication Data

Alcott, Louisa May, 1832-1888
Little women

Junior ed.
ISBN: 1-55013-414-0

I. Greenwood, Barbara, 1940–   II. Ruhl, Greg.
III. Title.

PZ7.A53Li 1992   j813'.4   C92-093225-8

Key Porter Books Limited
70 The Esplanade
Toronto, Ontario
Canada M5E 1R2

Typesetting: MacTrix DTP
Printed and bound in Hong Kong

92 93 94 95 96 6 5 4 3 2 1

1

"Christmas won't be Christmas without any presents," grumbled Jo, from where she lay on the rug.

"It's so dreadful to be poor." Meg smoothed the faded skirt of her old dress.

"I don't think it's fair for some girls to have plenty of pretty things, and other girls nothing at all," added little Amy, with an injured sniff.

"We've got Mother and Father and each other," Beth reminded them contentedly from her corner.

The four young faces brightened at the cheerful words, but darkened again as Jo said sadly, "We haven't got Father, and we won't have him for a long time." She didn't say "perhaps never," but each girl silently added it, thinking of Father far away, where the fighting was.

The fire crackling in the grate was the only sound

for a moment, then Meg spoke. "You know why Mother suggested not having any presents this Christmas; it's going to be a hard winter for everyone. She thinks we ought not to spend money for pleasure, when our men are suffering so in the army. We can't do much, but we can make some little sacrifices. We ought to do it gladly, but I'm afraid I don't." Meg sighed, thinking of all the pretty things she wanted.

"But what good would our little bit do? We've only got a dollar each. The army wouldn't be helped much by that. I agree not to expect anything from Mother and you, but I do want to buy *Undine*," said Jo, who was a bookworm.

"I'd like some new music." Beth sounded wistful.

"I shall get a nice box of Faber's drawing-pencils; I really need them," Amy said decisively.

"Mother didn't say anything about *our* money," Jo pointed out. "Let's each buy what we want and have a little fun; I'm sure we work hard enough."

"I know *I* do — teaching those tiresome children all day," began Meg.

"You don't have nearly as hard a time as I do," Jo broke in. "How would you like to be shut up all day with a nervous, fussy old woman. Never satisfied, always worrying at me 'til I'm ready to fly out the window."

"It's naughty to fret, but I do think washing dishes and keeping things tidy is the worst work in the world. My hands get so stiff I can't practice well at all." And Beth looked at her rough hands with a sigh.

"I don't believe any of you suffer as I do," cried Amy. "*You* don't have to go to school with impertinent girls who insult you because your nose isn't nice and laugh at your handed-down dresses."

Meg leaned over to stir the fire. "If only we had the money Papa lost when we were little. How happy and good we'd be if we had no worries."

"You said the other day the King children were always fighting and fretting in spite of all their money. We're happier than that."

"So we are, Beth. Even though we do have to work, we make fun for ourselves. We're a pretty jolly set, as Jo would say."

"Jo uses such slangy words." Amy looked disapprovingly at the long figure stretched out on the rug. Jo immediately sat up, put her hands in her pockets, and began to whistle.

"Don't, Jo. It's so boyish!"

"That's why I do it."

"I detest rude, unladylike girls."

"I hate affected, niminy-piminy chits!"

"Birds in their little nests agree," sang Beth.

"Really, girls, you are both to be blamed," said Meg, beginning to lecture in her elder-sister fashion. "You're old enough to leave off boyish tricks, Josephine. Now that you turn up your hair, you should remember you're a young lady."

"I'm not! And if turning up my hair makes me one, I'll wear it in two tails 'til I'm twenty," cried Jo, pulling off her net and shaking down her chestnut hair. "I hate to think I've got to grow up and be Miss March. I want so much to be a boy and go and fight alongside Papa, and all I can do is stay home and knit." Jo shook the blue army sock until the needles rattled like castanets and her ball of yarn bounded across the room.

"Poor Jo. It's too bad, but it can't be helped," said Beth, stroking the glossy head at her knee. "You must try to be contented with making your name boyish and playing brother to us girls."

"As for you, Amy," Meg resumed, "you're altogether too particular and prim."

"If Jo is a tomboy and Amy a goose, what am I, please?" asked Beth, ready to share in the lecture.

"You are a dear and nothing else," answered Meg warmly, and no one contradicted her, for "Mouse" was the pet of the family.

The sisters sat knitting away in the twilight, while the December snow fell silently outside and the fire crackled cheerfully within. The clock struck six. Beth swept the hearth and put a pair of slippers down to warm. The sight of the old shoes cheered everyone up.

Mother was coming. Meg lit the lamp. Amy got out of the easy chair without being asked, and Jo forgot how tired she was as she sat up to hold the slippers nearer to the blaze.

"These are quite worn out. Marmee must have a new pair."

"I thought I'd get her some with my dollar," said Beth.

"No, I shall!" cried Amy.

"I'm the oldest," Meg began, but Jo cut in.

"I'm the man of the family until Papa comes back, and I shall provide the slippers."

"I'll tell you what we'll do," said Beth. "Let's each get her something for Christmas, and not get anything for ourselves."

"That's like you, dear!" exclaimed Jo. "What will we get?"

Everyone thought for a moment, then Meg announced, as if the idea was suggested by the sight of her own pretty hands, "I shall give her a nice pair of gloves."

"Army slippers," cried Jo. "The best to be had."

"Handkerchiefs, all hemmed," said Beth.

"A bottle of cologne," added Amy. "It won't cost much, so I'll have some left to buy my pencils."

"We must go shopping tomorrow afternoon," said Jo, marching up and down with her hands behind her back. "And we must rehearse the play for Christmas night. Come here, Amy, and do the fainting scene. You're stiff as a poker in that."

"I can't help it; I've never seen anyone faint. And I don't choose to make myself all black and blue, tumbling flat the way you do. I shall fall into a chair gracefully."

"Do it this way. Clasp your hands and stagger across the room." And away went Jo, crying melodramatically, "Roderigo, save me! Save me!"

Amy followed, but she poked her hands out stiffly and said "Ow!" as tamely as though she had pricked her finger.

Jo gave a despairing groan. "Do the best you can. Don't blame me if the audience laughs. Come on, Meg."

The rehearsal went smoothly. Don Pedro defied the world for two pages without a break; Hagar, the witch, chanted awful incantations over her kettleful of simmering toads; Roderigo rent his chains asunder, and Hugo died with a wild "Ha! Ha!"

"The best we've had yet," said Meg, as the dead villain sat up and rubbed her elbows.

"You write such splendid things, Jo. You're a regular Shakespeare!" exclaimed Beth.

"Not quite," Jo replied modestly. "*The Witch's Curse* is rather nice, but I've always wanted to do *Macbeth*. 'Is that a dagger that I see before me?'" Jo rolled her eyes and clutched at the air.

"No, it's the toasting fork," Meg cried, and the rehearsal ended in a burst of laughter.

"Glad to find my girls so merry," said a cheery voice at the door. "How have you got on today? How is your cold, Meg? Jo, you look tired to death."

The girls rushed to take their mother's wet cloak and

bonnet. Beth pulled the chair close to the fire, Jo slipped the warm slippers on her mother's feet, and Amy climbed into her lap. Mrs. March settled down for a brief rest while the older three rushed between kitchen and parlor setting out the supper.

"I've got a treat for you," Mrs. March said as they finished the last of the biscuits.

"A letter. A letter!" Jo tossed up her napkin. "Three cheers for Father."

"Yes, a nice long letter. He's well and thinks he shall get through the cold season better than we feared."

"I do think it was splendid of Father to go as a chaplain when he wasn't strong enough to go as a soldier," said Meg warmly.

Jo jumped up and paced about the room. "Don't I wish I could go as a drummer so I could be near him and help him."

"It must be very disagreeable to sleep in a tent and eat all sorts of bad-tasting things." Amy made a face at the thought.

"When will he come home, Marmee?" asked Beth with a quiver in her voice.

"Not for many months, dear. He'll stay and do his work as long as he can. Now come and hear the letter."

They gathered around the fire, Mother in the big chair, the girls clustered about her. The letter was cheerful, telling of life in camp, marches, and military news. Only at the end did it overflow with longing for the family at home.

"'Give them my love and a kiss,'" Mrs. March read. "'Tell them I think of them by day and pray for them at night. A year seems a long time, but tell them while we wait we may all work so that these hard days will not be wasted. I know they will be loving children to you and do their duty so faithfully that when I come back I will be prouder than ever of my little women.'"

Everybody sniffed at that part. Even Jo wasn't ashamed of the great tear that dropped off the end of her nose. "I'll try to do my duty here instead of wanting to be somewhere else," said Jo, thinking that keeping her temper at home was a much harder task than facing a Rebel or two down south.

Amy hid her face in her mother's shoulder and sobbed. "I *am* selfish but I'll truly try to be better."

"We all will!" exclaimed Meg.

Beth said nothing, but wiped her tears away with the blue army sock and began to knit with all her might.

"Well, my dears, we must all of us try a little harder," agreed their mother. "Look under your pillows Christmas morning and you'll find something to help you."

2

Jo was the first to wake in the gray dawn of Christmas morning. No stockings hung from the mantle, and for a moment she felt disappointed. Then she remembered her mother's promise, and, slipping her hand under her pillow, drew out a little crimson-covered book. She knew it as soon she saw the familiar picture of the stable and the baby in the manger. She woke Meg with a "Merry Christmas" and urged her to look under her pillow. A green-covered book appeared, with the same picture. Soon Beth and Amy woke to rummage and find their little books — one dove-colored, the other blue.

"Girls," said Meg, looking from Jo to the little girls in the room beyond, "since Father went away and all this war trouble unsettled us, we've neglected many things. Mother wants us to remember the message in this story. I think we should read our books every day."

"How good Meg is!" Beth exclaimed. "Come, Amy, I'll help you with the hard words." And the room was very still while the pages were softly turned, and the winter sun crept in to touch the bright heads and serious faces with a Christmas greeting.

"Where is Mother?" asked Meg, half an hour later, as she and Jo ran downstairs to thank her for their gifts.

Hannah, who had lived with the family so long she was more friend than servant, was in the kitchen making breakfast. "Goodness only knows," she said, dropping biscuit dough into a pan. "Someone came to the door needing help and off she went. There never was such a woman for giving away vittles and clothes and kindlin'."

"She'll be back soon." Meg looked over the presents that had been collected in a basket and kept under the sofa, ready to be produced at the proper time. "Why, where is Amy's bottle of cologne?"

"She went off to put a ribbon on it, I think," replied Jo, dancing about the room to take the first stiffness out of the army slippers.

"How nice my handkerchiefs look." Beth held one out proudly, showing off the somewhat uneven embroidery along the edge.

"Bless the child! She's gone and put 'Mother' on them instead of 'M. March.' How funny!" cried Jo.

"Isn't that right? I thought it was better that way because Meg's initials are M.M. and I don't want anyone to use these but Marmee." Beth's eyes filled with tears.

"It's all right, dear," — Meg hugged her little sister as she frowned at Jo, — "and quite sensible. Now no one can mistake them."

"There's Mother. Hide the basket. Quick!" cried Jo as a door slammed. Steps sounded in the hall, but it was Amy, dressed in cloak and hood, who came in.

"Where have you been?" asked Meg.

"Don't laugh at me. I didn't mean for anyone to know. I went out to change the little bottle for a big one. I gave *all* my money to get it, and I'm truly trying not to be selfish anymore." As she spoke, Amy showed the handsome flask that replaced the cheap one. She looked so earnest that Meg hugged her on the spot, and Jo pronounced her a "trump."

"I'm so glad I changed it," Amy said, placing the stately bottle in the basket, "for mine is the handsomest present now."

Another bang of the street door sent the basket under the sofa again.

"She's coming!" cried Jo.

Beth ran to the piano and struck up her brightest march, Amy threw open the door, and Meg conducted her mother to the seat of honor. Mrs. March was both surprised and touched as she examined her presents. The slippers went on at once; a new handkerchief was slipped into her pocket, well scented with Amy's cologne; and the gloves were pronounced a "perfect fit."

After much laughing and kissing and explaining, the girls went off to prepare for the day's festivities. They had put their wits together to make whatever the play called for — guitars from cardboard, antique lamps from gravy boats covered in silver paper, old robes dressed up with shiny spangles, armor covered in the same useful diamond-shaped bits.

Jo played all the male parts and took immense satisfaction in a pair of russet leather boots given her by a friend who knew a lady who knew an actor. The smallness of the company made it necessary for the two principal actors to take several parts apiece. They were kept busy learning their lines, whisking in and out of various costumes, and managing the stage besides.

On Christmas night, a dozen neighborhood girls who had been invited as an audience piled onto the bed, which was the dress-circle, and sat before the blue and yellow chintz curtains in a most flattering state of expectancy. Rustlings and whisperings came from behind the curtain, with the occasional giggle from Amy. Then a bell sounded, the curtains flew apart, and the Operatic Tragedy began.

In a cave (some blankets thrown over a clothes-horse) in a gloomy wood (a few little plants in pots), a witch stirred something steaming in a black kettle. Suddenly, Hugo the villain stalked in, waving his sword and demanding a love potion. The witch chanted,

> *"Hither, hither from thy home*
> *Airy sprite, I bid thee come!*
> *Born of roses, fed on dew,*
> *Charms and potions canst thou brew?"*

In rushed Amy, waving a wand and singing,
> *"Hither I come.*
> *Take the spell and use it well*
> *Or its power will vanish soon."*

With much shouting and stamping of boots, shrieking and wringing of hands, the thrilling story was acted out. The curtain closed to wild applause from the audience, which bounced so enthusiastically that the cot-bed suddenly snapped closed and extinguished their applause. Both the villain and the witch flew to their rescue, and all were taken out unhurt, although several were speechless with laughter.

The excitement had hardly died down when Hannah appeared at the door. "Mrs. March's compliments, and would the ladies walk down to supper."

The actors and audience trooped downstairs and gazed at the table in rapturous amazement. Ice cream? Cake and fruit? French bonbons? And in the middle of the table a great bouquet of hothouse flowers! Never since the departed days of plenty had they seen such treats.

"Is it fairies?" asked Amy.

"It's Santa Claus," said Beth.

"Mother did it." Meg smiled through the gray beard she had not yet taken off.

"Aunt March had a good fit and sent it," cried Jo.

"All wrong," replied Mrs. March. "Old Mr. Laurence sent it."

"The Laurence boy's grandfather? What in the world put such an idea into his head? We don't know him," exclaimed Meg.

"He knew your grandfather years ago. He sent me a note this afternoon saying he hoped I would allow him to express his friendly feeling toward my children by sending a few trifles in honor of the day."

"That boy put it into his head, I know he did. I wish we could get acquainted. He looks as if he'd like to know us," said Jo, "but he's bashful, and Meg is so prim she won't let me speak to him when we pass." Jo handed the plates around as the ice cream began to melt.

"You mean the people who live in the big house next door?" asked one of the visitors. "My mother says old Mr. Laurence is very proud and doesn't like to mix with his neighbors. He keeps his grandson locked up and makes him study very hard."

"The boy brought the flowers himself," said Mrs. March. "I like his manners. He seems nicely brought up."

"He needs fun," said Jo decidedly. "I'm sure he does. And I mean to know him some day."

3

"Jo! Jo, where are you?" cried Meg, from the foot of the attic stairs.

"Here," answered a husky voice from above, and, running up, Meg found her sister wrapped in a comforter, eating apples and crying over a sad story. As Meg appeared, Jo shook the tears off her cheeks and waited to hear the news.

"Such fun! Look! An invitation for tomorrow night." Meg read from the card delightedly, "'Mrs. Gardiner would be happy to see Miss Meg and Miss Josephine March at a little dance on New Year's Eve.' What shall we wear?"

"You know we haven't got anything but our poplins," said Jo, her mouth full of apple.

"If only I had a silk," Meg sighed.

"I'm sure our pops look nice enough. At least, yours does. I forgot, there's a burn and a tear in mine. What shall I do?"

"You must sit all you can and keep your back out of sight. The front is all right. I shall have a new ribbon for my hair. My gloves are all right, I guess."

"Mine are spoiled with lemonade. I shall have to go without."

"You must have gloves," cried Meg. "Gloves are more important than anything else. You can't dance without them."

"Then I shall stay still. I don't care for all that sailing around."

"Can't you make them do?" Meg asked anxiously.

"I can hold them crumpled in my hand. No, I'll tell you what — we'll each wear a good one and carry a bad one."

"Your hands are bigger than mine . . ." Meg began. "Oh, all right. Just don't stain it or put your hands behind you or say 'Christopher Columbus!' will you?"

"Don't worry about me. I'll be as prim as can be. Now go and answer your note and let me finish this splendid story."

The next evening Meg and Jo stood at the door,

ready for the great treat. Meg's silvery dress had been freshened with lace frills. Jo's maroon was brightened with a white chrysanthemum. Each wore one nice glove and carried one soiled one. Meg's high-heeled slippers were tight, and Jo's nineteen hairpins all seemed to stick straight into her head, but both girls looked forward happily to the evening out.

"Have you both got nice pocket handkerchiefs?" Mrs. March asked as they stepped out the door. "Then have a good time and come away at eleven when I send Hannah for you."

Mrs. Gardiner, a stately lady, greeted them kindly and handed them over to the eldest of her six daughters. Meg knew Sallie and felt at her ease very soon, but Jo, who didn't care for girlish gossip, stood with her back against the wall and felt as much out of place as a colt in a flower garden.

Meg was asked to dance at once, and the tight slippers tripped about so briskly that none would have guessed the pain their wearer suffered smilingly. Jo saw a big, red-headed youth approach her corner and, fearing he meant to ask her to dance, slipped into a curtained alcove. As the curtain fell she found herself face to face with the "Laurence boy."

"I didn't know anyone was here," she stammered, preparing to back out.

The boy looked startled, but said, "Don't mind me. Stay if you like. I only came here because I don't know many people and I felt strange."

"So did I. Don't go away. Please — unless you'd rather."

The boy sat down and looked at his shoes.

"We had a good time over your nice Christmas present, Mr. Laurence."

"Grandpa sent it, Miss March."

"But you put the idea into his head, didn't you? And I am not Miss March, only Jo."

"Well, I'm not Mr. Laurence, only Laurie."

"What an odd name!"

"My first name is Theodore but the fellows at school called me 'Dora' so I made them call me 'Laurie' instead."

"How did you make them?"

"I thrashed them."

"Well, I can't thrash Aunt March to make her stop calling me Jos-y-phine, so I suppose I shall have to bear it."

"Don't you dance, Miss Jo?"

"I like it well enough if there is plenty of room. In a place like this I'd be sure to upset something. Don't *you* dance?"

"Sometimes. I've been abroad for a good many years and don't yet know how you do things here."

"Abroad!" cried Jo. "Oh, tell me! I dearly love to hear about people's travels."

Laurie didn't seem to know where to begin, but Jo's eager questions soon set him going. He told her how he had been at school in Switzerland, where the boys never wore hats and had a fleet of boats on the lake.

"Don't I wish I'd been there! Did you go to Paris?"

"We spent last winter there."

"I suppose you're going to college soon. I see you

pegging away at your books — no, I mean studying hard."
Jo blushed at the dreadful slang that had escaped her.

Laurie smiled, but didn't seem shocked. "Not for a
year or two. Not until I'm seventeen anyway."

"How I wish I was going to college."

"I shall hate it. I want to live in Italy and enjoy
myself in my own way."

Jo wanted very much to ask what his own way was,
but his black brows looked rather threatening as he knit
them, so she changed the subject. "That's a splendid
polka. Why don't you go and try it?"

"If you will come too," he answered gallantly.

"I can't. I told Meg I wouldn't because—"

"Because what?"

"You won't tell?" Jo looked undecided.

"Never."

"Well, I have a bad habit of standing before the fire,
and so I burn my frocks. This one is nicely mended, but
it shows. Meg told me to keep still so no one would see.
You may laugh if you want to."

But Laurie didn't laugh. "I'll tell you how we'll
manage it; there's a long hall out there. We can dance
grandly and no one will see us. Please come?"

Jo went gladly. Laurie taught her the German step,

which delighted Jo, being full of swing and spring. When the music stopped they sat down on the stairs to catch their breath. Laurie was in the midst of a story when Meg appeared in search of her sister. She beckoned, and Jo reluctantly followed her into a side-room.

"I've sprained my ankle," Meg said, sitting on the sofa and rubbing at her foot.

"Those silly shoes!" Jo exclaimed. "I can't see what you can do except call a carriage."

"That costs ever so much! I'll just wait here until Hannah comes. I'll make it home some way."

"Can I help?" asked a friendly voice, and there was Laurie with a cup of coffee and a dish of ice cream.

"Meg is tired and . . ."

"May I give these to your sister?" Laurie drew up a table, brought a second serving of coffee and ice cream for Jo, and they all sat down to a quiet game of "Buzz." Two or three other young people had joined the game by the time Hannah appeared. Meg forgot her foot and rose so quickly that she was forced to catch hold of Jo, with an exclamation of pain.

"Hush, don't say anything," she whispered, adding aloud, "I turned my foot a little, that's all." She limped upstairs to put her things on.

Hannah scolded, Meg cried, and Jo was at her wits' end until she decided to take things into her own hands. Slipping out, she ran downstairs and asked a servant if he could get her a carriage. Laurie, who had overheard, came up and offered his grandfather's carriage.

"It's so early. You can't mean to go yet." Jo felt relieved, but hesitated to accept the offer.

"I always go early — truly. Please let me take you home. I think it's raining out."

That settled it. After telling him of Meg's mishap, Jo gratefully accepted and rushed upstairs to bring down the rest of the party.

Laurie sat up on the box beside the driver so that

Meg could keep her foot up, and the girls were free to talk over their party.

"I had a capital time," said Jo, rumpling up her hair and making herself comfortable. "I saw you dancing with that redheaded man. Laurie and I had a good laugh, watching him do the polka. He looked like a grasshopper having a fit."

"That's very rude. He was quite nice. I enjoyed my dance. What were you doing, hiding away?"

Jo recounted her adventures and, by the time she had finished, they were home. With many thanks, they said "Good night" and crept in.

"I declare," Meg said when they had tiptoed up to their own room, "I feel like a fine young lady, coming home in a carriage and having a maid to wait on me."

Jo laughed as she rubbed her sister's swollen ankle with arnica. "I don't believe fine young ladies enjoy themselves a bit more than we do, in spite of our burned gowns and tight slippers that sprain our ankles when we're silly enough to wear them."

4

"What in the world are you doing now, Jo?" asked Meg one snowy afternoon, as her sister came tramping through the hall in rubber boots, old sack and hood, with a broom in one hand and a shovel in the other.

"Going out for exercise."

"I should think walking all the way to Aunt March's and back would have been enough. It's cold and dull out. Why don't you stay warm and dry by the fire, as I do."

"Never take advice. Can't keep still. Don't like to doze by the fire. I like adventures and I'm going to find some."

Meg went back to toast her feet and read *Ivanhoe*. Jo began to sweep paths with great energy. At the bottom of the garden a hedge separated the Marches' house from that of Mr. Laurence. One was an old, brown house, looking bare and shabby without the vines that covered it in summer; the other was a stately stone mansion. To Jo, this fine house seemed an enchanted palace.

At an upper window, Jo could see a black curly head leaning on a thin hand. Up went a handful of snow, and the head turned at once. Jo called out, "Are you sick? What are you doing to amuse yourself?"

Laurie opened the window and croaked out as hoarsely as a raven, "I've had a bad cold. Been shut up for a week. It's dull as a tomb up here."

"Shall I come up and read to you?"

"Yes, please!" The big eyes brightened.

"I'll ask Mother." Jo shouldered her broom and marched into the house.

Laurie was in a flutter of excitement at the idea of having company. Presently he heard a loud ring, then a decided voice asking for "Mr. Laurie." A surprised-looking servant ran up to announce the young lady, who appeared with her arms full.

"Here I am, bag and baggage," she said briskly. "Mother sends her love, Meg sent some blancmange for your sore throat, and Beth thought the kittens would be comforting."

"How kind you are. Please take a chair and let me do something to amuse my company."

"No, I came to amuse you. Shall I read aloud?" Jo glanced at a nearby shelf of books.

"Thanks. I've read all those. If you don't mind, I'd rather talk."

"I'll talk all day if you set me going. Beth says I never know when to stop."

"Is Beth the one who stays home a good deal? And the curly-haired one is Amy?" Laurie colored as Jo raised an eyebrow at him. "I hear you calling to each other in the yard," he explained. "And sometimes you leave the curtains open in the back room. I like to see you sitting around the table with your mother. I haven't got any mother, you know."

"We'll never draw the curtains again," Jo said warmly. "I give you leave to look as much as you like. We haven't been here a great while," Jo began cautiously, "but we

have got acquainted with all our neighbors but you."

"Grandpa is very kind, though he doesn't look it, but he does live among his books. And Mr. Brooke, my tutor, doesn't stay here, so I have no one to go about with me."

"You ought to make an effort and go everywhere you're invited. You won't be bashful long if you keep going, and then you'll have plenty of friends."

Laurie turned red again, but there was so much goodwill in Jo's voice that he couldn't take offense at being called bashful. After a little pause, during which he stared at the fire, he asked, "Do you like school?"

"Don't go to school. I'm a businessman — girl, I mean. I go to wait on my great-aunt."

Laurie opened his mouth to ask another question, then remembered it was rude to make too many inquiries into people's affairs. But Jo didn't mind having a laugh at Aunt March, so she gave him a lively description of that fidgety old lady, her fat poodle, and the parrot that talked Spanish. Laurie lay back and laughed until the tears ran down his cheeks.

"Oh, tell on, please," he said, taking his face out of the sofa cushion, red and shining with merriment.

Much elated by her success, Jo did tell on, all about

their plays and plans, their hopes and fears for Father, and the most interesting events of their little world. Then they got to talking about books.

"If you like them so much, come down and see ours. Grandpa's out, so you needn't be afraid," Laurie said, getting up.

"I'm not afraid of anything." Jo tossed her head.

"I don't believe you are." Laurie's voice showed his admiration, even though he privately thought she would have good reason to be afraid of the old gentleman in some of his moods.

When they reached the library, Jo clapped her hands and pranced, as she always did when especially delighted. The room was lined with books and pictures. A cozy chair was pulled up by the big, open fireplace.

"What richness!" Jo sighed, sinking into the chair. "Theodore Laurence, you ought to be the happiest boy in the world."

"A fellow can't live on books." Before he could say more, a bell rang, and Jo flew up, exclaiming, "Mercy me, it's your grandpa."

"What if it is?" Laurie laughed. "You're not afraid of anything!"

"I think I'm a little bit afraid of *him*, although I don't

really know why."

Just then a maid appeared in the doorway. "The doctor to see you, sir."

"Would you mind if I left for a minute? I suppose I must see him."

"Don't mind me. I'm happy as a cricket here." Jo browsed along the shelves, then stopped in front of a fine portrait of old Mr. Laurence. When the door opened again, she said, without turning, "I'm sure now that I shouldn't be afraid of him. His mouth is grim, but he's got kind eyes. He looks as if he has a tremendous will of his own. But I like him."

"Thank you, ma'am," said a gruff voice behind her, and there, to Jo's great dismay, stood old Mr. Laurence.

Jo blushed. She had a wild desire to run away. But that was cowardly, so she resolved to stay and get out of the scrape as best she could.

"So, you're not afraid of me, hey?" A quick look showed Jo the twinkling eyes under the bushy gray brows.

"Not much, sir."

"And I've got a tremendous will, have I?"

"I only said I thought so."

"But you like me in spite of it?"

"Yes, I do, sir."

The old gentleman gave a short laugh and shook hands with her. "What have you been doing to that boy of mine?"

"Only trying to be neighborly, sir." And Jo told how her visit came about.

"You think he needs cheering up, do you?"

"He seems a little lonely. We would be glad to give him some company, for we don't forget the splendid Christmas present you sent us."

"Tut, tut, tut. That was the boy's affair. Tell your mother I shall come and visit her some fine day. I should like to have a chat about my old friend, your grandfather. Well, well, there's the tea bell. Come down and go on being neighborly."

That was the beginning of many neighborly visits. At first the sisters had been shy of visiting as they were poor and Laurie rich. But, after a while, they found Mr. Laurence considered them the benefactors for befriending his lonely boy. They forgot their pride and exchanged visits happily. Even timid Beth overcame her fears and tripped joyfully over to the big house to play the wonderful piano.

5

"That boy is a perfect Cyclops, isn't he?" said Amy one day, as Laurie clattered by on horseback.

"What a thing to say," cried Jo. "He's got both eyes, and very handsome ones, too."

"I didn't say anything about his eyes. And I don't see why you have to fire up when I admire his riding."

"Oh my goodness, the little goose means a centaur." Jo burst out laughing.

"You needn't be so rude. You make mistakes, too. I just wish I had a little of the money Laurie spends on that horse."

"Why?" asked Meg, smiling.

"I'm dreadfully in debt."

"What on earth do you mean?"

"I owe at least a dozen pickled limes, and I don't

know how I'm going to pay them."

"Are limes the fashion now?"

"The girls are always buying them, and unless you want to be thought mean you must do it, too. Everyone is sucking them at their desks or trading them for pencils. If one girl likes another she gives her a lime. If she's mad at her she eats one before her face and won't even offer a suck. They treat by turns. I've had ever so many and I can't return them."

"How much will pay them off and restore your credit?" asked Meg, taking out her purse.

"A quarter would more than do it."

"Make this last as long as you can," her sister advised. "There isn't much more where that came from."

"Oh, thank you. It must be nice to have pocket money."

Next day at school Amy couldn't resist the temptation to display a moist brown-paper parcel before she tucked it into her desk. During the next few minutes the rumor spread that Amy March had twenty-four delicious limes and was going to treat. All the girls in Amy's set came flocking around. Katy Brown invited her to a party, Mary Kingsley insisted on lending Amy her watch to wear all morning, Jenny Snow offered to furnish answers for all the arithmetic questions. But Amy had not forgotten Jenny's comment just last week about "persons whose noses were not too flat to smell other persons' limes."

"You needn't be so polite all of a sudden, Jenny Snow," Amy said with disdain, "for you won't get any."

That morning a distinguished personage happened to visit the school, and Amy's beautifully drawn maps received praise. This honor caused Miss March to preen like a peacock, but it rankled in the soul of Miss Snow. No sooner had the guest bowed himself out than she decided on revenge.

"Please, sir," Jenny said, while Mr. Davis, the teacher, was marking her arithmetic, "Amy March has pickled limes in her desk."

Mr. Davis's yellow face flushed. He rapped on his desk with an energy that made Jenny skip to her seat with unusual rapidity.

"Young ladies, attention, if you please."

The buzz ceased. Fifty pairs of eyes were obediently fixed on his awful countenance.

"Miss March, come to the desk."

Amy rose with outward calm, but a secret fear oppressed her. What had she done?

"Bring with you the limes you have in your desk."

With a despairing glance at her friends, Amy obeyed.

"Now take these disgusting things four by four, and drop them out the window."

Scarlet with shame and anger, Amy went to and fro six dreadful times. Her friends flashed indignant or supplicating glances at the teacher's stern face. One passionate lime-lover burst into tears.

As Amy returned from her last trip, Mr. Davis said "Hem!" in his most impressive manner. "Young ladies, you remember what I said to you a week ago. No more limes. Miss March, hold out your hand."

Amy was shocked. Never in her life had she been struck. She put both hands behind her and turned pleading eyes on the teacher.

"Your hand, Miss March."

Amy clenched her teeth, threw back her head defiantly, and held out her hand for the stinging blows.

"You will stand on the platform until recess." The final disgrace! To face the whole school, the pitying eyes of her friends and the satisfied looks of her enemies, seemed unbearable. She fixed her eyes on the stove funnel to wait out the dreadful fifteen minutes.

Amy was in a sad state when she got home. When

the older girls arrived, an indignation meeting was held. Jo proposed that Mr. Davis be arrested at once. Meg bathed the insulted hand with glycerine. Mrs. March didn't say much, but she looked disturbed.

"You may stay home for a few days," Mrs. March said that evening. "I dislike Mr. Davis's manner of teaching and I think we shall find you another school."

"Good! I wish all the girls would leave and spoil his old school. It's perfectly maddening about those lovely limes."

"You broke the rules," her mother said firmly. "You deserved to be punished."

"You mean you're glad I was disgraced?"

"I don't approve of the means of punishment, but you're getting to be rather conceited, my dear, and it's time you set about correcting it. You have many little gifts, but there's no need to parade them about."

"Quite right," said Laurie, who was playing chess in a corner with Jo. "I know a girl who has a remarkable talent for music and she doesn't even know it."

"I wish I knew that girl," said Beth. "She might help me with *my* music."

"You do know her." Laurie looked at her with such mischievous meaning in his merry eyes that Beth suddenly turned red and hid her face in the sofa cushion.

When Laurie had gone Amy said, "Is Laurie an accomplished boy?"

"Yes, he has an excellent education and much talent," replied her mother.

"And he isn't conceited?"

"Not in the least. That's why he's so charming and we like him so much."

"I see," said Amy thoughtfully. "So it's nice to have accomplishments but not show off about them."

"Any more than it's proper to wear all your bonnets and gowns at once, so folks may know you've got them," said Jo, and the lecture ended in a laugh.

6

"The first of June! The Kings are off to the seashore tomorrow, and I'm free. Three months of vacation — how I shall enjoy it!" exclaimed Meg, coming home one warm day to find Jo stretched out on the sofa in an unusual state of exhaustion, while Beth took off her dusty boots, and Amy made lemonade for the refreshment of the whole party.

"Aunt March went off to Plumfield today, for which, oh, be joyful! I was mortally afraid she'd ask me to go with her. I quaked until she was in the carriage. Then, as it drove off, she popped out her head saying, 'Jos-y-phine, won't you—?' I basely turned and fled. Didn't stop 'til I was around the corner, where I felt safe."

"What shall you do all your vacation?" asked Amy.

"Lie late and do nothing," replied Meg from the

depths of the rocking chair.

"Too dozy for me," said Jo. "I shall improve the shining hours, reading on my perch in the old apple tree."

"Let's not do any lessons, Beth, just play all the time," Amy proposed.

"I *would* like to learn some new songs," Beth said. "And my dolls need new summer dresses."

"I propose a toast." Jo rose, glass in hand as the lemonade went around. "Fun forever, and no grubbing!"

The summer days passed pleasantly. One afternoon Beth came tripping into the house from her daily practice session on the piano at the Laurence house. "A nosegay for you, Marmee, from Laurie," she announced. "Miss Meg March, one letter and one glove."

"Why, I left a pair over there," Meg exclaimed, looking up from the wristband she was stitching. "How annoying to have an odd glove. My letter is only a German song I wanted. Mr. Brooke translated it, I think. This isn't Laurie's writing."

"A funny old hat for Jo," Beth continued, dropping a broad-brimmed straw hat on the table where her sister sat writing.

"That Laurie!" Jo exclaimed. "I said I was tired of burning my nose every hot day. He thinks I won't wear something so unfashionable, but I'll show him."

The next day another note arrived. In a big, dashing hand Laurie had written:

Dear Jo,
What ho! Some English girls and boys are coming tomorrow and I want to have a jolly time. I'll pitch my tent in Long-meadow and row the whole crew up to lunch and croquet. I want you all to come. Don't bother about rations — I'll see to that, only do come, there's a good fellow.

In a tearing hurry, yours ever,
Laurie

"Here's richness!" cried Jo, flying to tell the news to Meg.

"What do you know about these people?"

"Only that there are four. Kate is older than you. The twins, Fred and Frank, are my age, and Grace is nine or ten. Laurie knew them abroad. May we go, Mother? Mr. Brooke will be there, and Kate is old enough to play propriety for us girls."

The day of the picnic started with sunshine and laughter. Meg was glad to find that Kate Vaughan, though rich, was dressed simply. Jo took one look at her

and decided she didn't like Kate's stand-off-don't-touch-me air. Beth didn't feel quite so nervous of the boys when she found that Frank was shy and quiet. Amy and Grace stared at each other for a few minutes, then suddenly became bosom friends. They all set off together in two boats, Laurie and Jo rowing one, Mr. Brooke and Frank rowing the other, while Fred, the riotous twin, did his best to upset both by paddling about in a wherry like a demented waterbug.

Jo shouted "Christopher Columbus!" when she lost her oar, and Laurie said "My dear fellow did I hurt you?" when he tripped over her feet, taking his place. This exchange caused Miss Vaughan to raise her eyeglass and observe the two in a way that nettled Meg and made her wish Jo hadn't worn the old-fashioned straw hat Laurie had given her. Mr. Brooke caught her eye and smiled, and Meg felt he understood just what she thought of the haughty Miss Vaughan.

It was not far to Longmeadow. "Welcome to Camp Laurence!" cried the young host as they landed with exclamations of delight. The servants had already pitched the tent and set up the croquet wickets. Picnic baskets stood ready under the oak tree.

"Let's have a game before it gets hot, and then we'll see about dinner."

Beth and Frank sat under the tree to watch the other eight. Mr. Brooke chose Meg, Kate, and Fred. Laurie had Jo, Amy, and Grace. Both sides played vigorously, but a particular rivalry had sprung up between Jo and Fred. Jo was slightly ahead all the way. Then, at the last wicket, she missed her stroke. Fred's ball hit the wicket and stopped an inch on the wrong side. Running up to examine it, he gave the ball a sly nudge with his toe.

"I'm through! Now, Miss Jo, I'll settle you and get in first."

"You pushed it. I saw you," Jo said sharply. "That makes it my turn."

"Upon my word I didn't move it. Stand off, please, and let me have a go at the stake."

"We don't cheat in this part of the world," Jo said, angrily, "but *you* can if you choose."

Fred paid no attention, but swung at the ball, croqueting hers off across the meadow. Jo opened her lips to say something rude but contented herself with hammering down a wicket with all her might. Fred hit the stake triumphantly and declared himself out.

Jo went off to find her ball. She was a long time searching for it but, when she returned, she looked cool and quiet. The other side had nearly won, for Kate's ball was the last but one and lay near the stake.

"By George, it's all up with us," cried Fred excitedly. "Miss Jo owes me one, Kate. You're finished."

Jo looked at the two balls, then back at Fred. "In this part of the world, we believe in being generous to our enemies," she said. Then, leaving Kate's ball untouched, she won the game by a clever stroke.

Laurie threw up his hat, then remembered it

wouldn't do to exult over the defeat of his guests. He contented himself with whispering to Jo, "Good for you. He did cheat. I saw him. Won't do it again, I'll bet."

Under the pretense of pinning up Jo's braids, Meg whispered, "How good of you to keep your temper when he was being so provoking."

"Don't praise me, Meg. I could box his ears this minute. I had to stay down in the nettles 'til I knew I could hold my tongue."

"Time for lunch," said Mr. Brooke, looking at his watch. "Laurie, will you make the fire and get water? Miss March and Beth and I will spread the table. Jo, will you make coffee?"

After lunch, the younger ones lay under the tree, playing a quiet game of "Authors." Kate sat apart sketching.

"How beautifully you do it. I wish I could sketch," Meg said, sitting down beside her.

"Your mamma prefers other accomplishments, I fancy. So did mine, but I persuaded my governess to teach me. Can't you do the same with yours?"

"I have none."

"Ah, you go to school?"

"No, I am a governess myself."

"Oh, indeed," said Kate, but the tone of voice said, How dreadful! and made Meg wish she had not been so frank.

"Did the German song suit, Miss March?" inquired Mr. Brooke to fill in the awkward pause.

"Oh yes, it was very sweet and I am much obliged to whomever translated it."

"Do you not speak German, Miss March?"

"Not very well. My father taught me a little, but now that he's away I have no one to correct my accent."

Kate closed her sketchbook, and stood up. "I advise you to learn. German is a valuable accomplishment for teachers. I must go and see to Grace. She is romping."

"She rather turns her nose up at governessing, doesn't she?" Meg looked annoyed.

"There's nothing wrong with honest work, Miss Margaret."

"No, but I confess I sometimes find my pupils trying. I wish I liked it, as you do."

"Laurie is a good pupil. I shall be very sorry to lose him next year."

"What becomes of you when he goes to college?"

"I shall go off for a soldier. Every man is needed out there."

"Yes, I suppose so. But it's very hard for the mothers and sisters who stay home."

"I have neither. And few friends to care whether I live or die," Mr. Brooke said, rather bitterly.

"Laurie and his grandfather would care a great deal. And we should all be very sorry to have anything happen to you."

"Thank you." Mr. Brooke looked as though he might say more, but just then Grace and Amy came shrieking by, pretending they were riding horses. Then the others appeared, and an impromptu game of "Fox and Geese" finished off the afternoon.

7

Jo sat on the rickety sofa in the attic, her papers spread out on the old trunk, writing busily. The October day faded as she scribbled away. "There, I've done my best." She signed her name with a flourish and threw down her pen. Lying back, she read the manuscript through carefully, making dashes here and there, putting in many exclamation points; then she tied it up with a red ribbon, picked up a second manuscript, and crept quietly downstairs.

She put on her hat and coat as noiselessly as possible, then, creeping out the back door, took a roundabout way through the garden to the side street. Once there, she hailed an omnibus and rolled away to town, looking merry and mysterious. In the middle of town, she got off the bus and set off at a great pace until she came to a certain building on a busy street. She looked up the dirty staircase for a minute, then suddenly turned and walked quickly away. This maneuver she repeated several times, to the great amusement of a black-eyed young gentleman lounging in the window of the building opposite. On returning for the third time, Jo gave herself a shake, pulled her hat over her eyes, and walked up the stairs.

In ten minutes she came running back down the stairs with a very red face and the general appearance of a person who had just passed through a trying ordeal. When she saw the young gentleman waving to her, she looked cross and passed him with her head held high.

"Wait for me," Laurie called. "You're up to some mischief."

"So are you. What were you doing, sir, up in that billiard parlor?"

"Begging your pardon, ma'am, it's a gymnasium. I was taking a lesson in fencing."

"Oh, good. You can teach me and, when we play *Hamlet*, we'll make a fine thing of the sword fight."

"I'll teach you whenever you like, but don't think you'll distract me from your secret."

"I haven't got one," began Jo, but stopped suddenly, remembering that she had.

" 'Fess up, now, and then I'll tell you a very

interesting secret *I* know. I've been aching to tell it for ages. Come on, you begin."

"You won't tell anyone at home, will you?"

"Not a word."

"And you won't tease me in private?"

"I never tease."

"Yes, you do. You get everything you want out of people. You're a born wheedler. Well, anyway," Jo whispered. "I've left two stories with a newspaper man and he's to give me his answer next week."

"Hurrah for Miss March, the celebrated authoress!" cried Laurie, throwing up his hat and catching it again.

"Hush! It won't come to anything, I dare say, but I couldn't rest 'til I'd tried."

"It won't fail. Your stories are works of Shakespeare compared to half the rubbish published every day. Won't it be fun to see them in print?"

"What's *your* secret, Laurie? Play fair."

"Well — I may get into a scrape for telling, but I know where Meg's glove is."

"Is that all?" said Jo in disgust. "Well, where then?"

Laurie bent and whispered three words in Jo's ear. She stared at him for a minute, looking displeased, then walked on, saying sharply, "How do you know?"

"Saw it in his pocket."

"All this time?"

"Yes. Don't you like it?"

"Of course I don't. It's ridiculous. The idea of anyone coming to take Meg away! I don't think secrets agree with me. I feel rumpled up in my mind since you told me," Jo grumbled.

"Race down the hill with me and you'll feel better."

No one was in sight; the smooth road sloped invitingly, and the temptation was irresistible. Jo darted away, soon leaving hat and comb behind her and scattering hairpins as she ran.

"I wish I was a horse; then I could run forever in

this splendid air," Jo panted, dropping down under a maple tree at the bottom of the hill. "I hope no one sees me like this."

Just then Meg, looking particularly ladylike in her best afternoon dress, came along the street. She regarded her disheveled sister with well-bred surprise. "Jo, when will you stop such romping ways?"

"Never, 'til I'm old and stiff and have to use a crutch. Don't try to make me grow up before my time, Meg. It's hard enough seeing you change."

For the next two weeks, Jo behaved so strangely that her sisters were quite bewildered. She rushed to the door when the postman rang, was rude to Mr. Brooke, and would sit staring at Meg with a woebegone face. She and Laurie were always making signs at each other until the girls declared they had both lost their wits.

One afternoon, Jo bounced in with a newspaper in her hand. "Shall I read to you?" She looked at her sisters, who were all busy stitching. Then with a loud "Ahem" she began. The girls listened with interest.

"What a good story. Who wrote it?" Beth asked.

Jo suddenly sat up, cast away the paper, and, with a funny mixture of solemnity and excitement, announced, "Your sister."

"I knew it, I knew it." And Beth ran to hug her.

How delighted they all were to see "Miss Josephine March" actually printed in the paper, how proud Mrs. March was when she was shown.

"Tell us about it" — "When did it come?"— "How much were you paid for it?" cried the family, all in one breath.

So Jo recounted her tale of visiting the newspaper office. "He said he didn't pay beginners, only printed them so people could notice their stories, but Laurie says he'll see I get paid for the next ones. I'm so happy. Just think: in time I may be able to support myself and help all of you." Jo's breath gave out here and burying her face in the paper, she shed a few tears, for to be independent and to earn the praise of those she loved were the dearest wishes of her heart.

8

"November is the most disagreeable month in the whole year," said Meg, standing at the window one dull afternoon, looking out at the frost-bitten garden.

"That's the reason I was born in it," observed Jo, morosely.

"If anything pleasant should happen now," said Beth, "we should think it a delightful month."

"Well, nothing pleasant ever does happen in this family." Meg was feeling out of sorts and refused to be coaxed into a better mood. "We go grubbing along, day after day, without a bit of change and no fun."

"How blue we are!" cried Jo. "Don't I wish I could manage things for you as I do for my heroines. I'd have some rich relation leave you a fortune. Then you'd dash off in a blaze of elegance and splendor."

"People don't have fortunes left to them these days," said Meg bitterly. "It's a dreadfully unjust world."

"Jo and I are going to make fortunes for you all," said Amy, who sat in a corner, making little clay models of birds. "Just wait ten years, and see if we don't."

"Can't wait. And I haven't much faith in ink and dirt." Meg turned to the frost-bitten garden again. Jo leaned both elbows on the table.

"Two pleasant things *are* going to happen," insisted Beth, who sat at the other window. "Marmee is coming down the street, and Laurie is coming through the garden."

In they both came, Mrs. March with her usual question, "Any letter from Father, girls?" and Laurie to say, "Come for a drive. I've been working away at mathematics 'til my head is a muddle. I'm going to take Brooke home and blow the cobwebs out of my head. Will you come?"

A sharp ring at the door interrupted them. "A telegram, ma'am," Hannah said. "From Washington."

Mrs. March went white. She snatched it and read the two lines it contained:

> *Your husband is very ill.*
> *Come at once.*

As the girls gathered around their mother, breathless with anxiety, she said, "If only it isn't too late. I must think what to do. Laurie?"

"Here, ma'am. Let me help, too."

"Send a telegram saying I'll come at once. Then take a note to Aunt March." She tightened her lips and said, "I hate to ask, but I *must* borrow money from her for the journey. Jo, I must go prepared for nursing. Run to the shops and get these ointments for me. Beth and Meg, come and help me pack."

They all scattered like leaves before a gust of wind. As Meg ran through the entry hall with a pair of rubbers in one hand and a cup of tea in the other, she suddenly came upon Mr. Brooke.

"I'm very sorry to hear of this, Miss Margaret," he said in a kind, quiet tone. "I came to offer myself as escort to your mother. Mr. Laurence has commissions for me in Washington, and it would give me much satisfaction to be of service to her there."

"How kind you are! Mother will accept, I'm sure. Thank you very, very much."

Everything was arranged by the time Laurie arrived with the money from Aunt March, folded into a note in which she pointed out that she had always told them it was absurd for March to go into the army. Mrs. March read the note silently, then put it on the fire.

The short afternoon wore away. As Amy and Beth were putting tea on the table, Mrs. March said, "Where's Jo? It's getting late."

Just then the door slammed and Jo walked in with an odd expression on her face. She laid a roll of bills on the table.

"Twenty-five dollars! My dear, where did you get it?"

"It's mine, honestly. I only sold what was my own." As she spoke, Jo took off her bonnet.

"Your hair! My dear girl, there was no need for this."

"I was wild to do something for Father," said Jo. "I saw a sign in a barbershop saying they paid for hair long enough to make wigs and switches. It's my contribution toward making Father comfortable."

The next morning the four girls stood at the gate, waving as the carriage, carrying their mother and Mr. Brooke to the train station, turned the corner.

"It seems as if half the house is gone," Meg said forlornly.

"'Hope and keep busy' — that's our motto." Jo turned back to the house. "Let's see who will remember it best. I shall go to Aunt March. Won't she lecture though!"

"I shall go to the Kings', I guess, though I'd much rather stay and see to things here." Meg wished she hadn't made her eyes so red with crying.

"Beth and I can keep house perfectly well," said Amy with an important air.

"We'll have everything nice when you come home," added Beth, getting out her mop and dishpan.

For a week, the amount of virtue in the old house would have supplied the neighborhood. At first self-denial was all the fashion, then the girls began to fall back into the old ways. Jo caught a bad cold and was ordered to stay home. Aunt March did not like to hear people read with colds in their heads. Jo was happy to subside onto the couch and nurse her cold with a stack of books. Amy found that housework and art did not go well together and returned to her clay models. Meg went daily to her pupils and came home intending to mend and sew, but much of her time was spent writing long letters to Washington. All the forgotten duties were picked up by Beth, and everyone felt how sweet and helpful she was.

Ten days after Mrs. March's departure, Beth came in, carrying a basket. She took off her hooded cloak and sat down slowly at the kitchen table.

"Christopher Columbus!" cried Jo, looking at her

sister's red-rimmed eyes. "What's the matter?"

"My head aches and my throat hurts. I'm afraid I've got scarlet fever."

"Where could you possibly get that?"

"The family at the end of the street. Marmee always took them a little food and outgrown clothes, and I thought I should, too. The baby's been sick all week. The doctor was there today. They've all got scarlet fever, and he said I should go home and take belladonna or I'd be sick, too."

"No, you won't!" cried Jo, hugging her close. "If only Mother was home. I'll call Hannah. She knows about sickness."

"Don't let Amy come. She's never had it. Can you and Meg catch it again?"

"Guess not. Don't care. Serve me right, selfish pig, not to notice what you were doing. I should have gone myself."

Hannah took charge at once, assuring Jo that there was no need to worry, everyone got scarlet fever and, if treated right, no one died. "Now I'll tell you what we'll do," she said when she'd examined Beth, "we'll have Dr. Bangs, just to take a look at you, dear. We'll send Amy off to Aunt March to keep her out of harm's way, and one of you girls can stay home and help nurse."

"I shall stay, as I'm the eldest," began Meg.

"I shall, because it's my fault," insisted Jo. "I said I'd do all the errands and I didn't."

"Which will you have, Beth? There's no need of more than one," said Hannah.

"Jo, please."

"I'll go and tell Amy," said Meg, feeling a little hurt, yet relieved, on the whole, because she did not like nursing and Jo did.

Amy rebelled outright. Meg reasoned, pleaded, commanded: all in vain. She left in despair to ask Hannah what should be done. Before she came back,

Laurie walked into the parlor to find Amy sobbing.

"I don't wish to be sent off as if I was in the way," Amy said when she'd finished telling her story. She expected to be consoled, but Laurie only put his hands in his pockets and walked about the room, whistling softly. Presently he sat down beside her.

"Come and hear what a jolly plan I've got. You go to Aunt March's and I'll come by every day and take you out driving, and to the theater."

"But it's dull there, and Aunt March is so cross."

"It won't be dull with me popping in every day to tell you how Beth is."

"Will you bring me back the minute Beth is well?"

"On my honor as a gentleman."

"And take me to the theater, truly?"

"A dozen theaters."

"Well — I guess — I will."

"Good girl. Call Meg and tell her you give in." Amy felt annoyed about "giving in," but when Meg and Jo came running down to behold the miracle, she put on a sweet, self-sacrificing smile and promised to go.

"How is Beth?" asked Laurie.

"Lying down. She says she feels better, but Hannah looks worried. What a trying world it is!" cried Jo, rumpling up her hair in a fretful sort of way. "No sooner do we get out of one trouble than another comes down."

"Shall I telegraph your mother?"

"I think we ought to tell her if Beth is really ill, but Hannah says she can't leave Father and it will only make them anxious. Hannah knows what to do."

"Hum. Well, suppose you ask Grandfather after the doctor's been."

"Yes, that's what we'll do," decided Meg. "Jo, run and fetch Dr. Bangs."

"Stay where you are," said Laurie, taking up his cap. "I'm errand boy here."

Beth did have the fever and was much sicker than anyone but Hannah and the doctor suspected. Meg stayed home and kept house so Jo and Hannah could nurse the patient. But the fever fits grew worse and Meg begged to be allowed to write to their mother. Hannah insisted there was no danger yet. A letter from Washington settled the argument: Mr. March had had a relapse and could not think of coming home for a long while.

How dark the days seemed now, how sad and lonely the house, and how heavy were the hearts of the sisters as they worked and waited, while the shadow of death hovered over their once-happy home.

9

The first of December was a wintery day, a bitter wind blew, snow fell fast, and the year seemed to be getting ready for its death. When Dr. Bangs came that morning, he looked long at Beth, held a hot hand in both his own, then said in a low tone, "If Mrs. March *can* leave her husband, she'd better be sent for."

Hannah nodded without speaking, Meg dropped into a chair, Jo ran to the front hall and, throwing on her things, rushed out into the storm. When she returned from the telegraph office, Laurie was waiting in the parlor.

"A letter," he said, waving it at her. "Good news. Your father is on the mend."

"Thank goodness." Jo's face was so full of misery that Laurie asked quickly —

"What is it? Is Beth worse?"

"I've just sent for Mother," said Jo, tugging at her rubber boots. "The doctor told us to."

"Oh, Jo, it's not that bad, is it?"

"Yes it is. She doesn't know us, she doesn't talk to us, she doesn't even look like my Beth. And there's nobody to help us bear it." As the tears streamed down Jo's face, she reached out her hand, as if groping in the dark.

"I'm here. Hold on to me," Laurie whispered as well as he could with a lump in his throat.

And Jo did hold on. The warm grasp of the friendly human hand soothed her sore heart. Laurie longed to say something comforting, but no fitting words came. Soon Jo dried her tears and looked up with a grateful face.

"Thank you, Laurie. I'm better now."

"I'll tell you something that will make you feel even better." Laurie spoke very fast and turned red. "I telegraphed your mother yesterday. She'll be here tonight."

Jo grew quite white, then flew out of her chair and threw her arms around his neck, crying, "Oh, Laurie! Oh, Mother! I *am* so glad!"

Laurie, though decidedly amazed, patted her back soothingly until Jo, suddenly breathless, backed away saying, "Oh, that was dreadful of me. Bless you, Laurie.

Bless you." Then she vanished into the kitchen, where she told the cats she was "Happy, happy, happy!"

Laurie departed, feeling he had made rather a neat thing of it.

When Jo took the happy news up to the sickroom, everyone rejoiced but Beth. She lay in a heavy stupor, the once-rosy face vacant, the once-pretty hair rough and tangled on the pillow. All day she lay so, rousing only to mutter, through parched lips, "Water."

Jo and Meg hovered, watching, waiting, hoping. The doctor called in and said some change, for better or worse, would take place by midnight. The girls never forgot that night, for no sleep came to them as they kept watch.

"If God spares Beth, I'll never complain again," promised Meg.

"If life is as hard as this, I don't see how we shall ever get through it," added her sister despondently.

The clock struck twelve. The house was as still as death. Weary Hannah slept. The sisters watched Beth. A pale shadow seemed to fall on the little bed. An hour went by. They heard Laurie leaving for the train station. At two, Jo, who had been standing by the window thinking, heard a movement by the bed. She saw Meg kneeling with her face hidden in the covers. "Beth's dead," she thought and was beside the bed in an instant. The little face looked pale and peaceful. The fever flush and look of pain were gone. Just then Hannah appeared. She took Beth's hands, listened at her lips. "Her skin's damp," she whispered. "The fever's broke. She's sleeping natural. Oh, praise be!"

Never had the sun risen so beautifully and never had the world seemed so lovely as it did to the heavy eyes of Meg and Jo as they looked out in the early morning, when their long, sad vigil was done.

"Hark," cried Jo at the sound of bells below. A cry from Hannah, and then Laurie's joyful whisper, "She's home, girls. She's home."

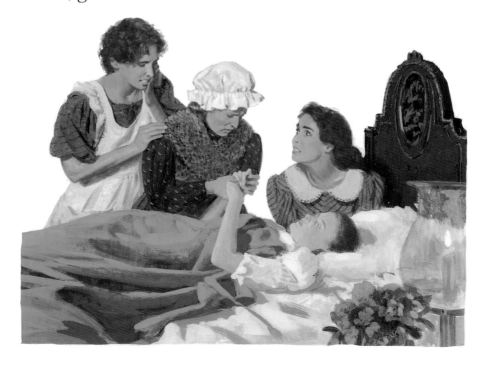

10

What a strange yet pleasant day that was. With a blissful sense of burdens lifted, Meg and Jo closed their eyes and lay at rest like storm-beaten boats safe at anchor. Mrs. March would not leave Beth's side, but rested in the big chair, waking often to brood over her child. Laurie posted off to comfort Amy and told his story so well that Aunt March never once said, "I told you so."

That evening, while Meg was writing to her father, Jo slipped upstairs to Beth's room.

"I want to tell you something, Mother."

"Beth is asleep," said Mrs. March, holding out her hand. "Speak low."

"It's about Meg." Jo settled herself on the floor at her mother's feet. "It's a little thing, but it bothers me. Laurie told me that Mr. Brooke keeps one of Meg's gloves in his waistcoat pocket. Laurie teased him about it, and Mr. Brooke owned that he liked Meg but didn't dare say so because she was so young and he was so poor. Now, isn't that a *dreadful* state of things?"

"Do you fancy Meg is interested in John?"

"Who?"

"Mr. Brooke. I fell into the way of calling him John at the hospital. He was perfectly open with us. He told us he loved Meg but would earn a comfortable home before asking her to marry him."

"I knew there was mischief brewing." Jo leaned her chin on her knees and shook her fist at the reprehensible John. "She was more interested in the reports he sent than she was in *your* letters."

"I'm sorry this happened so soon, for Meg is only seventeen, but it is natural that each of you will go to your own homes in time."

"Yes, but I'd planned for her to marry Laurie. Wouldn't that be nice?"

"Laurie is hardly grown up enough for Meg. Don't make plans, Jo. We can't meddle safely in other people's lives."

"But I hate to see things going all criss-cross and getting snarled up when a snip here and a pull there would straighten it out."

"Straighten what out?" Meg asked, tiptoeing into the room with the finished letter in her hand.

"Just one of my stupid speeches," Jo said, unfolding herself and stretching. "Coming to bed, Meg?"

Mrs. March, glancing over the letter said, "Please add that I send my love to John."

"Do you call him 'John'?"

"He was so devoted to your poor father that we couldn't help growing fond of him. It seemed natural to call him 'John' after all he had done for us." Mrs. March watched her daughter's face carefully, but the serene smile reassured her that Meg was not yet in love.

"I'm glad of that," Meg replied quietly. "He is so lonely. Good night, Mother. It is so comforting to have you here."

Jo watched Meg carefully for the next few days. "Doesn't eat, lies awake, mopes in corners," Jo reported to their mother in disgust. "Once, I caught her singing that song he gave her. Whatever shall we do?"

"Leave her alone," advised Mrs. March. "Be kind and patient." But Jo looked ready to try more violent measures.

Next day, Jo found a note lying on the front mat.

"How odd. It's for you, Meg." Mrs. March and Jo were deep in their own affairs when a sound from Meg made them look up.

"It's a mistake. He didn't send it. Oh, Jo, how could you?" And Meg hid her face in her hands, crying as if her heart was broken.

"Me? I've done nothing? What's she talking about?" Jo cried.

Meg's eyes kindled with anger as she pulled a crumpled note from her pocket and threw it at Jo. "You wrote it and that bad boy helped you. How could you be so mean and cruel?"

Jo and her mother hardly heard her for they were reading:

My dearest Margaret,
I can no longer restrain my passion and must know my fate
before I return. I dare not tell your parents yet, but I think
they would consent if they knew we adored one another. I
implore you to say nothing to your family, but send one word
of hope through Laurie to

Your devoted
John

"That villain!" cried Jo. "I'll fetch him over this minute to beg your pardon."

"Wait, Jo. You must clear yourself first," said her mother sharply. "You have played so many pranks—"

"On my word, Mother, I never saw that note before. I should think you'd know," she said, turning on her sister, "that Mr. Brooke would never write such stuff."

"It's like his writing," faltered Meg, comparing it with the note in her hand.

"Oh Meg, you didn't answer it?" cried Mrs. March.

"Yes, I did." And Meg hid her face in her hands.

"Here's a scrape. Let me bring that wicked boy over—"

"Hush, let me manage this," commanded their mother. "Tell me the story, Meg."

"Laurie gave me this first note. I worried about it but" — Meg blushed — "I wanted to keep my little secret, just for a bit. I wrote only that I was too young and didn't wish to have any secrets from you. Now he writes that he sent no such letter and he's sorry that my roguish sister Jo should take such liberties with our names. Oh, how am I ever going to face him!" Meg wailed, hiding her face in her mother's lap.

Jo tramped the room, calling Laurie names. All of a sudden she stopped, caught up the two notes and, after looking closely at them, said decidedly, "Laurie wrote *both* these letters. He kept teasing me about having a secret and, when I wouldn't tell him, he guessed it was about Meg and thought up this scheme to pay me back. Just wait 'til I drag him over here."

Away ran Jo, and Mrs. March gently told Meg Mr. Brooke's real feelings.

"I've been so scared and worried," Meg confessed. "I don't want to have anything to do with lovers. If John *doesn't* know anything about this, make Jo and Laurie hold their tongues. I *won't* be deceived and plagued and made a fool of."

The instant Laurie's step was heard in the hall, Meg fled into the study, and Mrs. March received the culprit alone. Jo was dismissed but chose to march up and down the hall like a sentinel, fearing that the prisoner might bolt. When they were called in, Laurie was standing by their mother. He reached his hands out penitently.

"I'll never tell him. Wild horses won't drag it out of me. Please forgive me, Meg. I know I don't deserve to be spoken to for a month, but you will, though, won't you?"

Meg pardoned him, and Mrs. March's grave face relaxed, but Jo stood aloof. Laurie looked at her once or twice, but, as she showed no sign of relenting, he made a low bow to the others and walked off without a word.

As soon as he had gone, Jo wished she had been more forgiving. After a while she yielded to impulse and, armed with a book to return, went over to the big house.

"He's shut up in his room and won't see no one," the maid informed her.

Up went Jo and knocked smartly on the door of Laurie's study.

"Stop that, or I'll come out and make you." The tone was threatening.

Jo immediately knocked again; the door flew open, and in she bounced before Laurie could recover from his surprise. Seeing that he really was out of temper, Jo assumed a contrite expression and said meekly, "I came to make up and can't go away 'til I have."

"Don't be a goose."

"What's the matter?"

"I've been shaken and I won't bear it!" growled Laurie indignantly.

"By your grandfather?" she asked, and when Laurie nodded curtly, "Why?"

"Because I wouldn't say what your mother wanted me for. I would have told my part but I couldn't without bringing Meg in. So I held my tongue and put up with the scolding until he collared me. Then I got angry and bolted."

"What pepperpots you are! Now Laurie, be sensible."

"Don't preach. If he doesn't trust me, then there's no point in staying here. I've got lots of money. I'll go to Washington and see Brooke. Why don't you come, too? Surprise your father."

For a moment Jo looked as if she would agree; such a wild plan just suited her. "Don't tempt me, Laurie. If I get your grandpa to apologize for shaking you, will you give up running away?"

"Yes, but you won't."

"If I can manage the young one, I can manage the old one," muttered Jo, as she walked away, leaving Laurie bent over a railway map.

Mr. Laurence was in the library. His shaggy eyebrows flew up when he saw her. "What's that boy been up to?" he barked. "Out with it. I won't be kept in the dark." He looked so alarming that Jo would gladly have run away, but she made herself brave it out.

"Indeed, sir, I can't tell. Mother forbade it. But he's

asked pardon and been punished quite enough."

"Hum — ha — well, if the boy held his tongue because he promised and not out of obstinacy, I'll forgive him. He's a stubborn fellow. Hard to manage."

"So am I, but a kind word will govern me when all the king's horses and all the king's men couldn't," said Jo.

"You think I'm not kind to him, hey?"

"Oh, dear, no. You are too kind and then a trifle hasty when he tries your temper."

"Well, what the dickens does the fellow expect?"

"If I were you, I'd write him an apology, sir. That will make him feel foolish and he'll come down quite amiable."

Mr. Laurence gave her a sharp look and put on his spectacles, saying slowly, "You're a sly puss but I don't mind being managed by you and Beth. Here, give me a bit of paper and let's have done with this nonsense."

Everyone thought the little matter was now ended and the cloud blown over, but the mischief was done. Meg never alluded to a certain person, but she thought of him a good deal and dreamed dreams more than ever.

11

Beth improved rapidly. Soon she was able to lie on the study sofa, amusing herself with the cats. Jo took her for an airing each day, carrying her around the house in her strong arms. Meg cheerfully baked goodies for "the dear," and Amy celebrated her return home by giving away as many of her treasures as she could prevail on her sisters to accept.

Christmas approached rapidly. Hannah "felt in her bones" it was going to be a grand day. To begin with, Beth felt uncommonly well that morning and was able to stand at the window to behold the offering from Jo and Laurie.

Out in the garden stood a stately snow-maiden, crowned with holly, bearing a basket of fruit and flowers in one hand, a great roll of music in the other, and, around her chilly shoulders, a perfect rainbow of an Afghan. How Beth laughed when she saw it, how Laurie ran up and down to bring in the gifts, and what ridiculous speeches Jo made as she presented them!

"I'm so full of happiness that, if only Father were here, I couldn't hold one more drop," said Beth, quite sighing with contentment as Jo carried her off to the study to rest.

Half an hour later, Laurie opened the parlor door and popped his head in. "Here's another Christmas present for the March family."

When a tall man, muffled up to the eyes, leaning on another tall man, appeared in the doorway, there was a general stampede. Mr. March disappeared in the embrace of four pairs of loving arms. Jo disgraced herself by nearly fainting away; Mr. Brooke kissed Meg entirely by mistake, as he stammeringly explained; Amy the dignified tumbled over a stool and, never stopping to get up, hugged her father's boots. Then the study door opened, and Beth flew straight into her father's arms.

There never was such a Christmas dinner as they had that day. The fat turkey was a sight to behold, stuffed, browned, and decorated; the jellies glistened

and the plum pudding steamed. "Which is a mercy," said Hannah, "for my mind was that flustered it's a miracle I didn't roast the pudding and boil the turkey."

The Laurences dined with them, as did Mr. Brooke, at whom Jo glowered darkly, to Laurie's amusement. The two invalids sat in easy chairs at the head of the table, and the whole company toasted healths, told stories, sang songs, and had a thoroughly good time.

"Just a year ago we were groaning over the dismal Christmas we expected to have. Do you remember?" asked Jo.

"Rather a pleasant year on the whole," said Meg,

congratulating herself on having treated Mr. Brooke with dignity.

"I think it's been a pretty hard one," observed Amy.

"Rather a rough road," her father agreed. "But you have got on bravely, my little women."

"How do you know?" asked Jo. "Did Mother tell you?"

"Straws show which way the wind blows, and I've made several discoveries today." He took up one of Meg's hands and pointed to a burn. "I remember when your one concern was to keep these hands white and smooth. I'm proud to shake this good, industrious little hand. And, Jo, I don't know whether the shearing sobered our wild sheep but I do know that in all Washington I couldn't find anything beautiful enough to deserve the twenty-five dollars sent by my good girl."

Jo's thin face grew rosy in the firelight.

"Now Beth," said Amy, longing for her turn, but ready to wait.

"There's so little of her I'm afraid she will slip away forever, but she's not as shy as she used to be. I'm just thankful to have you safe, my Beth."

After a minute's silence, he looked down at Amy, who sat on a stool at his feet. Stroking the shining head, he said, "I observed that Amy ran errands for her mother all afternoon and that she doesn't fret or look in the glass as much. I think she has decided to mold her character as carefully as she molds her clay figures."

"What are you thinking, Beth?" Jo asked, when Amy had thanked her father.

"It's singing time and I want to be at my old place." So sitting at her little piano, Beth sang a quaint old hymn her father had always loved:

"I am content with what I have,
Little be it or much;
And, Lord! contentment still I crave,
Because Thou savest such."

Wonderful as Christmas Day had been, the March family seemed restless as the days slipped by. Amy said, "Everyone seems to be waiting for something, which is strange since Father is home."

Laurie went by one afternoon and, seeing Meg at the window, fell down on one knee in the snow, tore his hair, and clasped his hands imploringly.

"What *does* the goose mean?" said Meg, trying to look unaware.

"He's showing you how your John will go on by and by. Touching isn't it?" answered Jo scornfully.

"Don't say *my John*. It isn't proper or true." But Meg's voice lingered over the words. "Besides I can't say anything 'til he speaks, and he won't because I'm too young."

"If he did speak, you wouldn't give him a good, decided 'no.' "

"I'm not so silly and weak as you think. I've got it all planned out. I should say quite calmly, 'Thank you, Mr. Brooke, but I agree with Father. I am too young. Let us be friends, as we were.' Then I should walk out of the room with dignity."

Meg rose as she spoke, and was just going to rehearse the dignified exit, when a step in the hall made her fly to her seat.

"Good afternoon. I came to see how your father finds himself today." Mr. Brooke's eyes went straight to Meg, who blushed and began sewing as though her life depended on it.

"Right this way," said Jo firmly, ushering the reluctant Mr. Brooke out.

As Meg sat stitching away in the parlor, unsure whether to bless Jo or not, Aunt March came hobbling in.

"There you are, Margaret. Just the girl I wanted to see. What's all this I hear about you and this Rook or Cook? You know it's your duty to make a rich match and help your family."

"Father and Mother don't think so; they like John, even though he *is* poor."

"He knows you've got rich relations. That's the secret of his liking, child."

"How dare you say such a thing! My John wouldn't marry for money, any more than I would. We are willing to work and we mean to wait. I'm not afraid of being poor, and I know I shall be happy with John because I know he loves me, and I—"

Meg stopped there, remembering all of a sudden that she hadn't made up her mind.

"I wash my hands of the whole affair," Aunt March proclaimed angrily. "And just remember, if you marry this Rook, not one penny of my money will you get."

"I shall marry whom I please, Aunt March, and you can leave your money to anyone you like," Meg said with a resolute air.

"Highty-tighty, miss! Let's hope Mr. Book can take care of you." And slamming the door in Meg's face, Aunt March drove off in high dudgeon.

"Thank you for defending me," a quiet voice said behind Meg. "And thanks to Aunt March for proving you do care for me."

"I didn't know how much until she abused you," Meg began, blushing as John took hold of her hands.

Fifteen minutes after Aunt March's departure, Jo came softly into the room. The scene that met her eyes sent her rushing wildly upstairs. "Do something, somebody!" she exclaimed tragically, bursting in on the invalids. "John Brooke is behaving dreadfully, and Meg likes it."

Mr. and Mrs. March left the room at speed, and Jo threw herself on the bed to scold tempestuously as she told the awful news to Beth and Amy. The little girls, however, thought it a most interesting event. Jo hoped for more sensible conversation from Laurie, but that young man came prancing in, overflowing with good spirits and bearing a huge bouquet for "Mrs. John Brooke," and saying, "I knew Brooke would get his own way; he always does when he makes up his mind to anything."

Later, following Jo into the parlor where the rest of the family were greeting Mr. Laurence, Laurie said, "You don't look very festive, ma'am; what's the matter?"

"I've lost my dearest friend," Jo sighed.

"You've got me."

"You are always a great comfort to me, Laurie," returned Jo, shaking hands gratefully.

"Well, now, don't be dismal, there's a good fellow. Meg is happy. Grandpa will see Brooke is settled into some job or other. I shall be through college in three years, and we'll go abroad. Wouldn't that console you?"

"There's no knowing what may have happened by then."

"True. Don't you wish you could take a look forward and see where we'll be?"

"I might see something sad. Everyone looks so happy now, I don't believe it could be much improved." And Jo's eyes brightened as she looked slowly around the room. Father and Mother sat together, talking quietly. Amy was drawing the lovers, who sat apart in a world of their own. Beth lay on her sofa, talking cheerily to her old friend, Mr. Laurence. Jo lounged in her favorite low seat, and Laurie, leaning on the back of her chair, his chin on a level with her curly head, smiled at her in the glass which reflected them both.